W9-AJS-436

Bink
&
gollie

JAN 2013

Bink & Gollie

Kate DiCamillo and Alison McGhee

illustrated by Tony Fucile

Candlewick Press

Text copyright © 2010 by Kate DiCamillo and Alison McGhee
Illustrations copyright © 2010 by Tony Fucile

All rights reserved. No part of this book may be reproduced, transmitted, or stored in an information retrieval system in any form or by any means, graphic, electronic, or mechanical, including photocopying, taping, and recording, without prior written permission from the publisher.

First edition 2010

Library of Congress Cataloging-in-Publication Data

DiCamillo, Kate.
Bink and Gollie / Kate DiCamillo and Alison McGhee ; illustrated by Tony Fucile. – 1st U.S. ed.
p. cm.
Summary: Two roller-skating best friends – one tiny, one tall – share three comical adventures involving outrageously bright socks, an impromptu trek to the Andes, and a most unlikely marvelous companion.
ISBN 978-0-7636-3266-3
[1. Friendship – Fiction. 2. Adventure and adventurers – Fiction. 3. Humorous stories.]
I. McGhee, Alison, date. II. Fucile, Tony, ill. III. Title.
PZ7.D5455Bi 2010
[Fic] – dc22 2009049100

11 12 13 14 15 16 WOR 10 9 8 7 6 5 4 3

Printed in Stevens Point, WI, U.S.A.

This book was typeset in Humana Sans.
The illustrations were done digitally.

Candlewick Press
99 Dover Street
Somerville, Massachusetts 02144

visit us at www.candlewick.com

For Karla Marie Rydrych, friend of my heart

K. D.

To Cindy Schultz Sykes, marvelous companion of my youth

A. M.

To Karen and Nina

T. F.

Contents

Don't You Need a New Pair of Socks?

"Hello, Gollie," said Bink.
"What should we do today?"
"Greetings, Bink," said Gollie.
"I long for speed."

"Let's roller-skate!"

ECCLES' EMPIRE OF ENCHANTMENT
BARGAIN BONANZA OF THE DAY: OUTRAGEOUSLY BRIGHT SOCKS! DON'T YOU NEED A NEW PAIR OF SOCKS?
BOOKS
BOOK SALE

MATT'S HOBBY
READERS'
Books

"I *do* need a new pair of socks!" said Bink. "Let's go inside."

"Hello," said Bink. "I'm here for the socks."

"Aisle ten," said Mr. Eccles.
"Aisle ten," said Mrs. Eccles.

"All righty, then," said Bink.
"Aisle ten."

1
Free!
POPCORN
5¢
25¢

"It's a sock bonanza!" said Bink.

"Indeed it is," said Gollie. "An extremely bright sock bonanza."

"I'll take this pair," said Bink.

"Bink," said Gollie, "the brightness of those socks pains me. I beg you not to purchase them."

"I can't wait to put them on," said Bink.

"I love socks," said Bink.

"Some socks are more lovable than others," said Gollie.

"I especially love bright socks," said Bink.

"Putting on socks is hard work," said Bink. "I'm hungry."

“Maybe Gollie is making pancakes.”

"Hello, Gollie," said Bink.
"Do I smell pancakes?"

"You do not," said Gollie.

"Will I smell pancakes?"
said Bink.

"Perhaps a compromise is in order, Bink," said Gollie.

"What's a compromise?" said Bink.

"Use your gray matter, Bink," said Gollie. "You remove your outrageous socks, and I will make pancakes."

"The problem with Gollie," said Bink, "is that it's either Gollie's way or the highway."

"My socks and I have chosen the highway."
"The problem with Bink," said Gollie, "is her unwillingness to compromise."

"Greetings, Bink," said Gollie. "I am eating pancakes. What are you doing?"

"I'm wearing my socks," said Bink.

"I have brought you half of my pancakes," said Gollie.
"And I've removed one of my outrageous socks," said Bink. "It's a compromise bonanza!"

P.S. I'll Be Back Soon

"It has been far too long since my last adventure," said Gollie. "I must journey forth into the wider world. But where?

"Tasmania? Timbuktu?"

"The finger has spoken," said Gollie.

To whom it may concern: I am on a journey. Thus, I am unable to answer the door.
P.S. I'll be back soon.

"I'm baffled," said Bink.
"Am I 'whom'?"
KNOCK,
KNOCK,
KNOCK!

"I cannot talk right now," said Gollie.

"Why not?" said Bink.

"Because," said Gollie, "I am high in the pure air of the Andes Mountains."

"All righty, then," said Bink.

"I wonder if Gollie's home yet," said Bink.

"Hmm," said Bink.

KNOCK,

KNOCK,

KNOCK!

“Please,” said Gollie. “Have you not read the sign?”

“I read it,” said Bink. “Aren’t you hungry?”

“Not at all,” said Gollie.

“Not even a little?” said Bink.

“Not even a little,” said Gollie.

"Not even a bit hungry!" said Bink.
"I don't believe it."

"What does *implore* mean?" said Bink.

KNOCK,
KNOCK,
KNOCK!

"Bink," said Gollie, "you must let me journey."
"But I brought you a sandwich," said Bink.

Bink: I implore you, do not knock.

"Here I am," said Gollie, "where none but a few have ventured. What an extraordinary accomplishment."

"Bink!" said Gollie. "Come see."

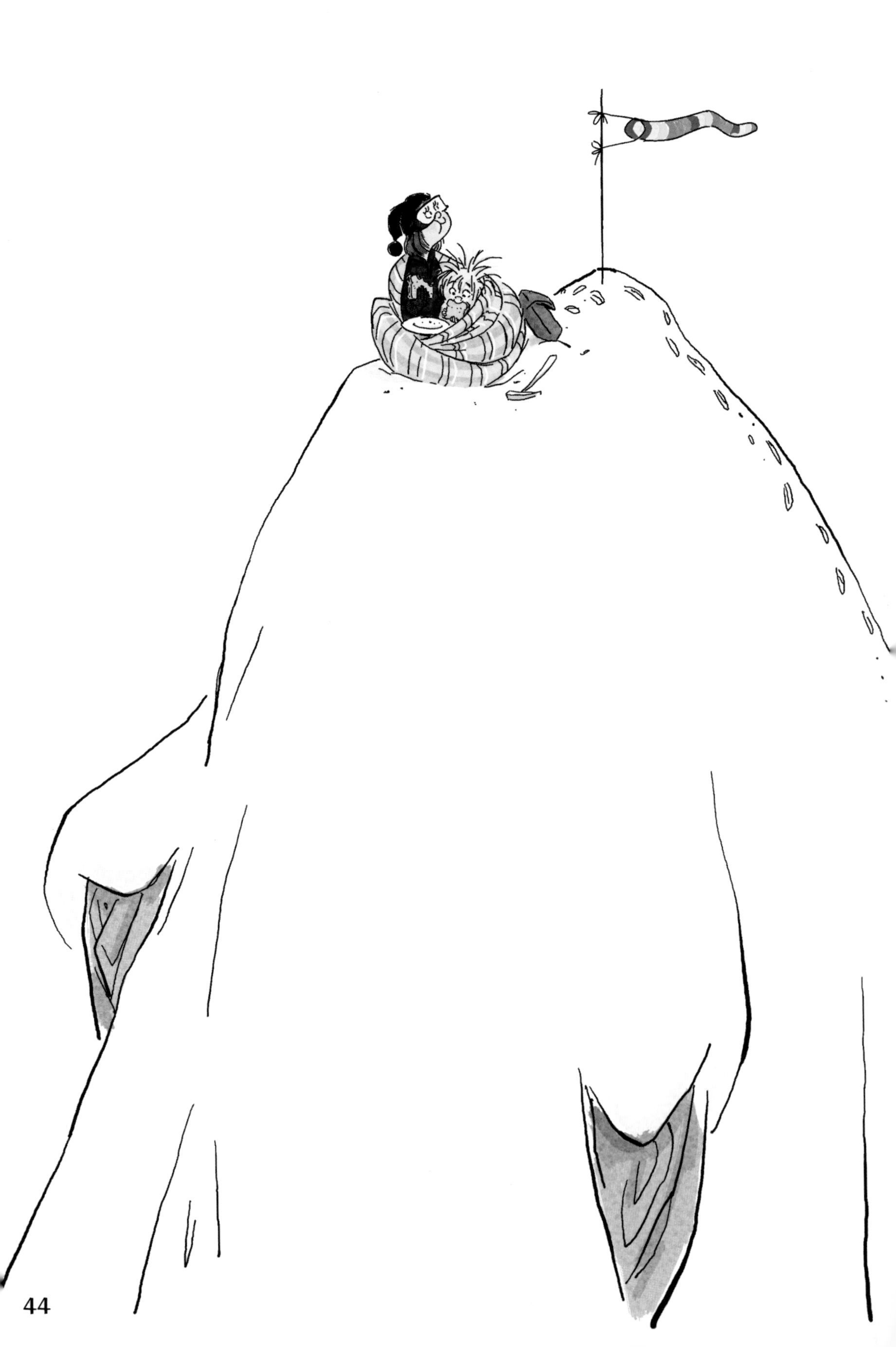

Give a Fish a Home

OPEN YOUR HEART TO A HOMELESS FISH!
FISHMAN'S
TROPICAL FISH
These Fish need your HELP!
OPEN
Give a Fish a Home!
PARK

"As you can see," said Mr. Fishman, "these are truly remarkable fish. Spectacular in virtually every way. Marvelous companions, marvelous. Each one desperate for a good home."

"I'll take that one," said Bink.

"Bink," said Gollie, "I must inform you that you are giving a home to a truly unremarkable fish."

"I love him," said Bink.

"Furthermore," said Gollie, "that fish is incapable of being a marvelous companion."

"I wonder what his name is," said Bink.

"Greetings, Bink," said Gollie. "Would you like to join me for pancakes?"
"Fred and I are on our way," said Bink.

"Fred?" said Gollie.
"Yes, Fred," said Bink. "My marvelous companion."

"I only made enough pancakes for two," said Gollie.

"Fred can share with me," said Bink.

"I only have two chairs," said Gollie.

"Oh, Fred doesn't need a chair," said Bink.

"Gollie, do you want to go see *Mysteries of the Deep Blue Sea*?" said Bink.

"Is that the movie about the fish?" said Gollie.

"It is!" said Bink. "It's the movie about the fish."

"Fred thinks that was a top-quality fish film." said Bink.

"I'm not sure I agree," said Gollie.

"Fred has a great idea," said Bink.

"I am almost afraid to inquire," said Gollie.

"Fred wants to roller-skate," said Bink. "Fred longs for speed."
"Fish know nothing of longing," said Gollie.

"Some fish do," said Bink. "Some fish long."

"Hey!" said Bink. "Wait up
for me and Fred!"

"Don't be afraid, Fred," said Bink.

"Oh, no," said Bink.

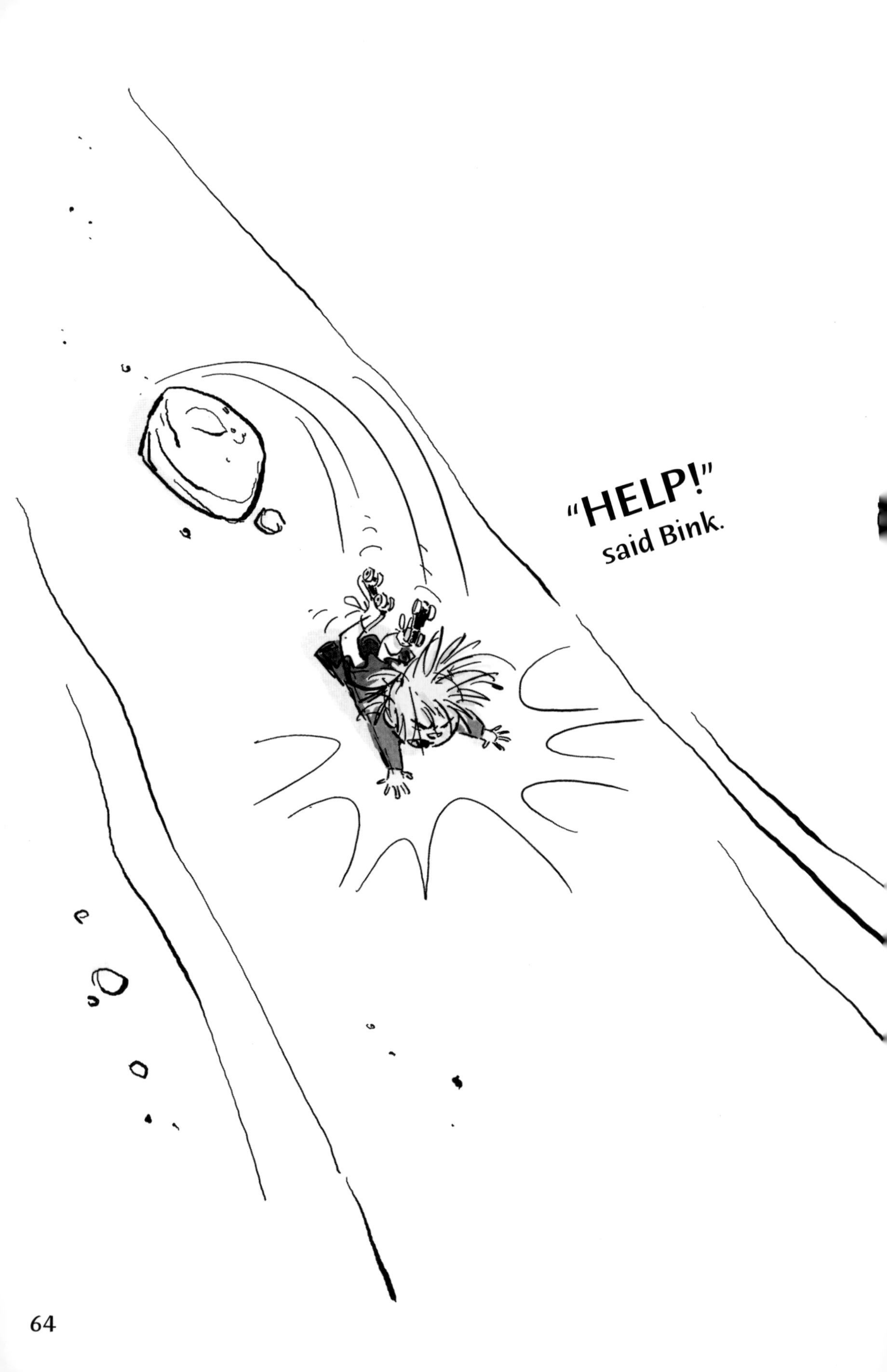
"HELP!"
said Bink.

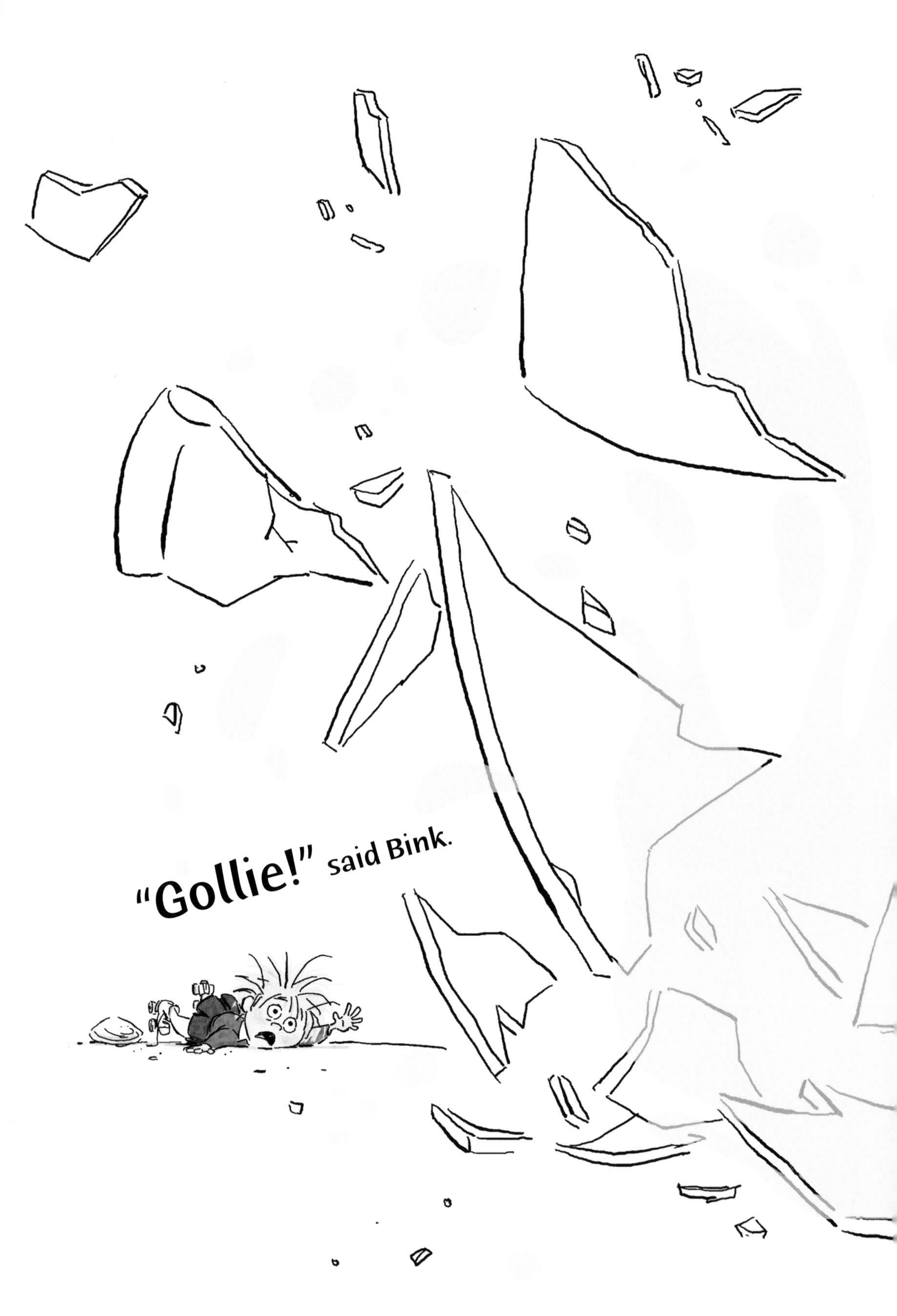
"Gollie!" said Bink.

"What are you doing?"

"Step aside," said Gollie.

"Wait!" said Bink. "Where are you going?"

"Help! Give me back my fish!"

"What have you done with Fred?" said Bink.

"I have saved Fred's life," said Gollie.

"How can Fred be my marvelous companion if he's in the pond?" said Bink.

"You can come and visit him," said Gollie. "If you feel the need of a marvelous companion."

"I think you're jealous of Fred," said Bink.

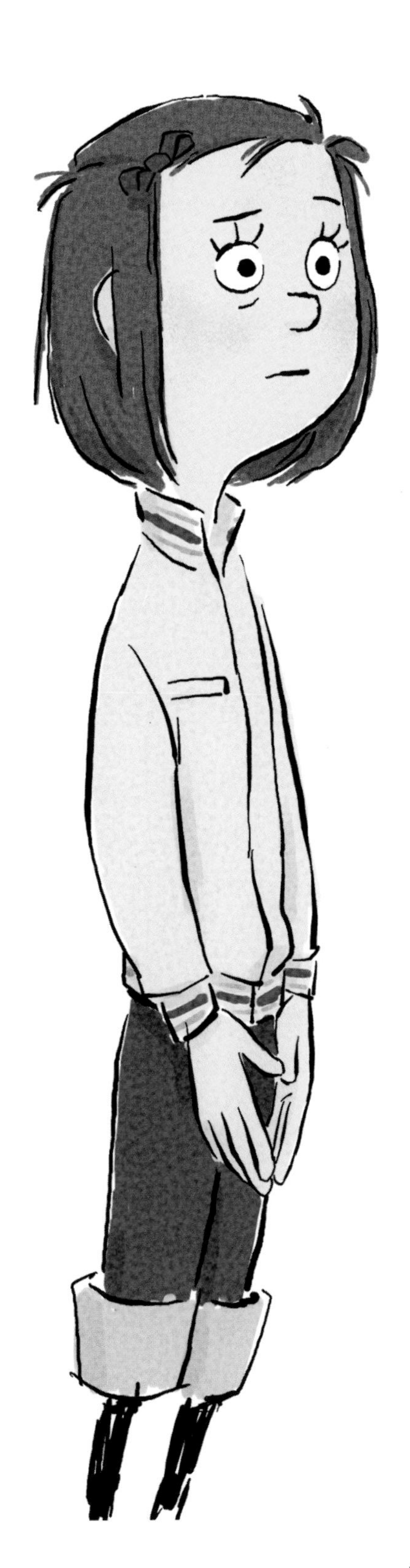

"Gollie," said Bink, "use your gray matter. Don't you know that you are the most marvelous companion of all?"

"Really?" said Gollie.

"Really," said Bink.

Six months later . . .